WHY FATHER CHRISTMAS WAS LATE FOR HARTLEPOOL

For Delia Huddy with love. D.H.
For Diana with love. S.H.

First published 1993
1 3 5 7 9 10 8 6 4 2
Text © 1993 Diana Hendry
Illustrations © 1993 Sue Heap

Diana Hendry and Sue Heap have asserted their rights
under the Copyright, Designs and Patents Act, 1988
to be identified as the author and illustrator of this work

First published in Great Britain
by Julia MacRae
an imprint of Random House
20 Vauxhall Bridge Road, London SWlV 2SA

Random House Australia (Pty) Ltd
20 Alfred Street, Milsons Point, Sydney, NSW 2061, Australia

Random House New Zealand Ltd
18 Poland Road, Glenfield, Auckland, New Zealand

Random House South Africa (Pty) Ltd
PO Box 337, Bergvlei 2012, South Africa

Random House UK Limited Reg. No 954009

A CIP catalogue record for this book is
available from the British Library

ISBN 1 85681 108 5

Printed in China

WHY FATHER CHRISTMAS WAS LATE FOR HARTLEPOOL

DIANA HENDRY
with illustrations by Sue Heap

Julia MacRae Books

LONDON SYDNEY AUCKLAND JOHANNESBURG

All four of them sat on the window-sill in the empty attic, waiting.

"While we're waiting," said One-Eyed Penguin, "we could play a game."

"I've forgotten what we're waiting for," said Knitted Owl.

"The child, of course!" said Albapot. "We're waiting for the child. The child who needs us."

"Oh yes," said Owl, making his eyes roll in a wise kind of way. "Only I've forgotten what the child looks like."

There was a long silence.

"A child has four legs, furry ears and a squawk," said Raggy Christine.

"Don't be stupid," said Albapot. "The child is nothing like that. The child has spots and a long neck and makes no noise at all."

"No," said One-Eyed Penguin, "Raggy is right. The child squawks."

"I'm tired of waiting," said Raggy Christine. "I want to go home."

"And where, when eggs have feathers, is home?" asked Albapot.

"Home is Once-Upon-a-Time," said Raggy Christine.

"Have you looked in the cupboard recently?" asked Penguin. "Perhaps the child came while we were asleep?"

"No," said Owl. "I looked this morning."

"I'm fed up," said Albapot. "Let's play hopscotch."

There was lots of space in the empty attic for hopscotch. Raggy Christine won because she had the best legs for hopping. Owl only had woolly stumps, Penguin's large flat flippers kept flapping on the lines, and Albapot's legs were loose so that she often fell over.

After the game Penguin helped Owl to put back his stuffing of old socks. This was always painful for Owl. He flitted back to the window-sill to recover his dignity.

"I was knitted," said Owl, "in the year 1905."

"I'm glad you remember something," said Albapot.

"And I know my address," said Owl. "It's The Attic, Potter's Bar."

"How long have we been here?" asked Penguin.

"Forever and ever amen," said Owl. "Long ago and far away we were left behind."

Penguin joined Owl on the window sill and gazed one-eyedly down at the street.

"It's Christmas time again," he said. "I can see the Christmas trees in the windows."

"Perhaps we'll get a child for Christmas," said Raggy Christine.

"Why do you get everything wrong?" asked Albapot. "*We* don't get a child for Christmas. The child gets *us*."

"Have you noticed," said Penguin, "that there's a sign outside our house?"

"Yes," said Raggy Christine. "I saw it yesterday. It says SOUL."

"What a fool you are!" said Albapot. "If you combed your hair you could see properly. It doesn't say SOUL. It says SOLD."

"What's that mean?" asked Penguin.

"I remember SOLD," said Owl.

"Well...?" said Albapot. "Go on."

"It means the OLD people have gone, SO ... So ... So ..."

"So new people are coming!" said Penguin. "With a child!"

"Oh!" cried Raggy Christine, tossing her yellow wool hair. "That's like my dream."

"You and your dreams," scoffed Albapot, and she gave one woollen strand a hard tug.

"Tell us," said Penguin. "I like a dream."

"It was about the child," said Raggy Christine. "A new child came and there were three kings. They sang a song. They sang, 'We three kings of merriment are.'"

"And?" said Albapot.

"That's all," said Raggy Christine.

"I don't think much of that!" said Albapot.

Suddenly there was an awful noise on the roof above their heads. Raggy Christine ran to Owl and hid her head in his soft knitted side.

"I think the house is falling down!" cried Penguin.

"It could be the window cleaner," said Owl nervously. "I remember the window cleaner. He climbed a ladder one day and washed the sky."

There was more clattering and banging on the roof and then a great rumbling tumbling noise inside the house. Penguin covered his ears with his flippers.

"Something's falling down the chimney," sobbed Raggy Christine.

"I expect it's an albatross," said Albapot lightly.

Then they heard footsteps.

"Play dead!" instructed Owl.

All four of them huddled on the window-sill and played dead. They heard the sound of heavy boots coming up
ONE FLIGHT
                    TWO FLIGHTS
                                        THREE FLIGHTS
of stairs. The attic door creaked slowly open.

"Evening all!" said Father Christmas.

Owl, Penguin, Raggy Christine and Albapot opened their eyes.

"Who? Who?" hooted Owl and felt very surprised at himself because he'd remembered his hoot.

"You must remember me," said Father Christmas. "I'm Father Christmas. Where is she then?"

"Who? Who?" hooted Owl again for he was in a state of owl-shook-shock.

"The child, of course," said Father Christmas, brushing the hair out of Raggy Christine's eyes. "I've got her on my list. Lily Peppermint, six months, five days, twenty-three hours and two minutes old. Moving to The Attic, Potter's Bar on Christmas Eve."

Don't
forget
List

pack
my
over
night
case

R's
cake
and
nuts

Extra
sack of
toys
for

Hartlepool
children
Remember
A-Z!

("Told you I knew my address," Owl whispered proudly to Penguin.)

"There must be a hold-up on the motorway," said Father Christmas. "Now the question is, should I wait on the roof or come back later? I've got some very nice toys for Lily but..." and he looked at them all, lined up hopefully on the window sill, "I expect she'll like you better. You're sort of child-friendly, aren't you?"

"We are! We are!" cried Owl, Penguin and Raggy Christine.

"We're rather battered, if that's what you mean," said Albapot.

"And loved. You all look very loved," said Father Christmas.

"Once upon a long time ago," said Raggy Christine.

"I think I'll come back later," said Father Christmas.

But just then they all heard noises downstairs.

A key in the lock. The front door opening. Voices in the hall. A deep voice. A light voice. A squawk.

"The child!" whispered Raggy Christine. "The child!"

"What am I going to do?" groaned Father Christmas. "They can't find me here. I can't be seen!"

"Quick. Hide in the cupboard!" said Albapot.

"Dear, oh dear, I'll be late for Hartlepool," said Father Christmas, squeezing himself into the cupboard.

"And his sack! His sack!" screeched Penguin in an awful flippery flap.

Together Albapot and Raggy Christine heaved the sack into the cupboard. And only just in time. For at that moment the attic door opened and the light went on. Owl, Penguin, Raggy Christine and Albapot lay in a dazed jumble on the floor.

"This will be her room," said the woman and she sat down on the window-sill with the child in her arms. "I always said that when I had a child, she'd have her bedroom in the attic."

"Looks as if she's got some toys already," said the man, picking Penguin up by one flipper. "Look at this old thing."

"He needs a new eye," said the woman.

"And this," said the man, picking Owl up by one foot.

"A knitted patch," said the woman.

Albapot was next. The man waggled her legs. "She needs a new elastic band," he said. "And I suppose you think this one needs a hair cut." He passed Raggy Christine to the woman.

The woman stroked Raggy Christine's woolly head.

"Squawk!" said the child.

Raggy Christine almost fainted with delight.

"Bring the cot up," said the woman.

"All the way up here?" said the man. "Tonight?"

"Yes," said the woman. "Every child should sleep close to the stars. Particularly on Christmas Eve. My mother told me so."

"Your mother!" said the man, but he went downstairs to fetch the cot.

It was way past midnight when the man and the woman went downstairs and left Lily Peppermint fast asleep in her cot with a sock hung at the bottom.

Father Christmas looked very pale when Raggy Christine and Albapot let him out of the cupboard.

"Chimneys, yes. Cupboards, no," said Father Christmas and he put a rattle, a boat for the bath, a chocolate mouse and a yellow bonnet in Lily Peppermint's sock.

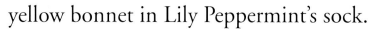

He sat Knitted Owl, One-Eyed Penguin, Raggy Christine and Albapot at the foot of the cot and then he took off his boots and crept downstairs. He was just about to climb back up the chimney when he had a thought. He tiptoed to the door of the man and woman's room and there he left two knitting needles, a ball of wool, one penguin's eye, a comb and an elastic band.

"Well," said Owl, when they knew by the rattle on the roof that Father Christmas was off to Hartlepool. "Well and well and well. *Now* I remember!"

"Next to a penguin," said Penguin, "this child is the most beautiful creature I've ever seen."

Very softly Raggy Christine began to sing. "We three kings of merriment are," she sang.

"Silly," said Albapot in quite a kindly way. "Can't you count? There are four of us."